HORRID HENRY'S
MONSTER MOVIE

Meet HORRiD HENRY
the laugh-out-loud
worldwide sensation!

* Over 15 million copies sold in 27 countries and counting

* # 1 chapter book series in the UK

* Francesca Simon is the only American author to ever win the Galaxy British Book Awards Children's Book of the year (past winners include J. K. Rowling, Philip Pullman, and Eoin Colfer).

"A loveable bad boy."

—People

"Horrid Henry is a fabulous antihero...**a modern comic classic**." —*Guardian*

"**Wonderfully appealing to girls and boys alike**, a precious rarity at this age." —Judith Woods, *Times*

"The best children's comic writer."
—Amanda Craig, Times

"**I love the Horrid Henry books by Francesca Simon**. They have lots of funny bits in. And Henry always gets into trouble!" —Mia, age 6

"My two boys love this book, and **I have actually had tears running down my face and had to stop reading because of laughing so hard**." —T. Franklin, parent

"**Fine fare for beginning readers**, this clever book should find a ready audience." —*Booklist*

"**The angle here is spot-on, and reluctant readers will especially find lots to love about this early chapter book series**. Treat young readers to a book talk or read-aloud and watch Henry go flying off the shelf." —*Bulletin of the Center for Children's Books*

"I have tried out the Horrid Henry books with groups of children as a parent, as a babysitter, and as a teacher. **Children love to either hear them read aloud or to read them themselves**." —Danielle Hall, teacher

"A flicker of recognition must pass through most teachers and parents when they read Horrid Henry. **There's a tiny bit of him in all of us**." —Nancy Astee, *Child Education*

"**As a teacher...it's great to get a series of books my class loves**. They go mad for Horrid Henry." —teacher

"**Short, easy-to-read chapters will appeal to early readers, who will laugh at Henry's exaggerated antics and relate to his rambunctious personality**." —*School Library Journal*

"**An absolutely fantastic series and surely a winner with all children. Long live Francesca Simon and her brilliant books! More, more please!**" —parent

"**Laugh-out-loud reading for both adults and children alike**." —parent

"**Henry's over-the-top behavior, the characters' snappy dialogue, and Ross's hyperbolic line art will engage even the most reluctant readers—there's little reason to suspect the series won't conquer these shores as well**." —*Publishers Weekly*

Horrid Henry by Francesca Simon

HORRID HENRY'S MONSTER MOVIE

Francesca Simon
Illustrated by Tony Ross

sourcebooks
jabberwocky

Text © Francesca Simon 2012
Cover and internal illustrations © Tony Ross 2012
Cover and internal design © 2012 by Sourcebooks, Inc.

Published by Sourcebooks Jabberwocky, an imprint of Sourcebooks, Inc.
P.O. Box 4410, Naperville, Illinois 60567-4410
(630) 961-3900
Fax: (630) 961-2168
www.jabberwockykids.com

Originally published in Great Britain in 2012 by Orion Children's Books.

Library of Congress Cataloging-in-Publication data is on file with the publisher.

Source of Production: Versa Press, East Peoria, Illinois, USA
Date of Production: August 2012
Run Number: 18382

Printed and bound in the United States of America.
VP 10 9 8 7 6 5 4 3 2 1

For Emily Lethbridge

CONTENTS

HORRID HENRY'S MONSTER MOVIE

Horrid Henry loved scary movies.
He loved nothing more than curling
up on the comfy black chair with a
huge bag of popcorn and a Fizzywizz
drink and jumping out of his seat in
shock every few minutes. He loved
wailing ghosts, oozing swamps, and
bloodthirsty monsters. No film was too
scary or too creepy for Horrid Henry.
MWAHAHAHAHAHAHA!

Perfect Peter hated scary movies. He
hated nothing more than hiding behind

the comfy black chair covering his eyes and jumping out of his skin in shock every few seconds. He hated ghosts and swamps and monsters. Even Santa Claus saying "ho ho ho" too loudly scared him.

Thanks to Peter being the biggest scaredy-cat who ever lived, Mom and Dad would never take Henry to see any scary movies.

And now, the scariest, most frightening, most terrible film ever was in town. Horrid Henry was desperate to see it.

"You're not seeing that movie and that's final," said Mom.

"Absolutely no way," said Dad. "Much too scary."

"But I love scary movies!" shrieked Horrid Henry.

"I don't," said Mom.

"I don't," said Dad.

"I hate scary movies," said Perfect Peter. "Please can we see *The Big Bunny Caper* instead?"

"NO!" shrieked Horrid Henry.

"Stop shouting, Henry," said Mom.

"But everyone's seen *The Vampire Zombie Werewolf*," moaned Horrid Henry. "Everyone but me."

Moody Margaret had seen it and said it was the best horror movie ever.

Fiery Fiona had seen it three times. "And I'm seeing it three more times," she squealed.

Rude Ralph said he'd run screaming from the cinema.

AAAARRRRGGGGHHHHHH.

Horrid Henry thought he would explode he wanted to see *The Vampire Zombie Werewolf* so much. But no. The movie came and went, and Horrid Henry wailed and gnashed.

So he couldn't believe his luck when Rude Ralph came up to him one day at recess and said:

"I've got *The Vampire Zombie*

Werewolf on DVD. Want to come over and watch it after school?"

Did he ever!

Horrid Henry squeezed onto the sofa between Rude Ralph and Brainy Brian. Dizzy Dave sat on the floor next to Jolly Josh and Aerobic Al. Anxious Andrew sat on a chair. He'd already covered his face with his hands. Even Moody Margaret and Sour Susan were there, squabbling over who got to sit in the armchair and who had to sit on the floor.

"Okay, everyone, this is it," said Rude Ralph. "The scariest movie ever. Are we ready?"

"Yeah!"

Horrid Henry gripped the sofa as the eerie piano music started.

There was a deep, dark forest.

"I'm scared!" wailed Anxious Andrew.

"Nothing's happened yet," said Horrid Henry.

A boy and a girl ran through the shivery, shadowy trees.

"Is it safe to look?" gasped Anxious Andrew.

"Shhh," said Moody Margaret.

"You shhh!" said Horrid Henry.

"MWAHAAAAHAAAAHAHAHAA!" bellowed Dizzy Dave.

"I'm scared!" shrieked Anxious Andrew.

"Shut up!" shouted Rude Ralph.

The pale girl stopped running and turned to the bandaged boy.

"I can't kiss you or I'll turn into a zombie," sulked the girl.

"I can't kiss *you* or *I'll* turn into a vampire," scowled the boy.

"But our love is so strong!" wailed the vampire girl and the zombie boy.

"Not as strong as me!" howled the werewolf, leaping out from behind a tree stump.

"AAAAAAAARRRRGGGHHH!" screeched Anxious Andrew.

"SHUT UP!" shouted Henry and Ralph.

"Leave her alone, you walking bandage," said the werewolf.

"Leave him alone, you smelly fur ball," said the vampire.

"This isn't scary," said Horrid Henry.

"Shh," said Margaret.

"Go away!" shouted the zombie.

"You go away, you big meanie," snarled the werewolf.

"Don't you know that two's company and three's a crowd?" hissed the vampire.

"I challenge you both to an arm-wrestling contest," howled the werewolf. "The winner gets to keep the arms."

"Or in your case, the paws," sniffed the vampire.

"This is the worst movie I've ever seen," said Horrid Henry.

"Shut up, Henry," said Margaret.

"We're trying to watch," said Susan.

"Ralph, I thought you said this was a really scary movie," hissed Henry. "Have you *actually* seen it before?"

Rude Ralph looked at the floor.

"No," admitted Ralph. "But everyone said they'd seen it and I didn't want to be left out."

"Margaret's a big fat liar too," said Susan. "She never saw it either."

"Shut up, Susan!" shrieked Margaret.

"Awhooooooo," howled the werewolf.

Horrid Henry was disgusted. He could make a *much* scarier movie. In fact…what was stopping him? Who better to make the scariest movie of all time than Henry?

How hard could it be to make a movie?
You just pointed a camera and yelled,
"Action!" Then he'd be rich rich rich.
He'd need a spare house just to stash all
his cash. And he'd be famous too.
Everyone would be begging for a role in
one of his mega-horror blockbusters.
Please can we be in your new monster movie?
Mom and Dad and Peter would beg.
Well, they could beg as long as they
liked. He'd give them his autograph, but
that would be *it*.

Henry could see the poster now:

HENRY PRODUCTIONS PRESENTS:

THE UNDEAD DEMON MONSTER WHO WOULD NOT DIE

Starring HENRY as the Monster

Written and Filmed and Directed by HENRY

"I could make a *really* scary movie," said Henry.

"Not as scary as the movie *I* could make," said Margaret.

"Ha!" said Henry. "Your scary movie wouldn't scare a toddler."

"Ha!" said Margaret. "*Your* scary movie would make a baby laugh."

"Oh yeah?" said Henry.

"Yeah," said Margaret.

"Well, we'll just see about that," said Henry.

Horrid Henry walked around his yard, clutching Mom's camcorder.

He could turn the yard into a swamp… flood a few flower beds…rip up the lawn and throw buckets of mud at the windows as the monster squelched his monstrous way through the undergrowth, growling and devouring, biting and—

"Henry, can I be in your movie?" said Peter.

"No," said Henry. "I'm making a scary monster movie. No nappy babies."

"I am not a nappy baby," said Peter.

"Are too."

"Am not. Mom! Henry won't let me be in his movie."

"Henry!" yelled Mom. "Let Peter be in your movie or you can't borrow the camcorder."

Gah! Why did everyone always get in his way? How could Henry be a

great director if other people told him
who to put in his movie?

"Okay, Peter," said Henry, scowling.
"You can be best boy."

Best boy! That sounded super. Wow.
That was a lot better than Peter had
hoped.

"Best boy!" shouted Horrid Henry.
"Get the snack table ready."

"*Snack* table?" said Peter.

"Setting up the snack table is the most
important part of making a movie," said
Henry. "So I want cookies and chips and

Fizzywizz drinks—NOW!" he bellowed. "It's hungry work making a movie."

Filmmaking next door at Moody Margaret's house was also proceeding slowly.

"How come I have to move the furniture?" asked Susan. "You said I could *be* in your movie."

"Because *I'm* the director," said Margaret. "So *I* decide."

"Margaret, you can be the monster in *my* movie. No need for any make-up," shouted Horrid Henry over the wall.

"Shut up, Henry," said Margaret. "Susan. Start walking down the path."

"BOOOOOOOOOOOOO," shouted Horrid Henry. "BOOOOOOOOOOOOO."

"Cut!" yelled Margaret. "Quiet!" she screamed. "I'm making a movie here."

15

★ ★ ★

"Peter, hold the flashlight and shine the spotlight on me," ordered Henry.

"Hold the flashlight?" said Peter.

"It's very important," said Henry.

"Mom said you had to let me *be* in your movie," said Peter. "Or I'm telling on you."

Horrid Henry glared at Perfect Peter.

Perfect Peter glared at Horrid Henry.

"Mom!" screamed Peter.

"Okay, you can be in the movie," said Henry.

"Stop being horrid, Henry," shouted Mom. "Or you hand back that camera instantly."

"I'm not being horrid; that's in the movie," lied Henry.

Perfect Peter opened his mouth and then closed it.

"So what's my part?" said Peter.

16

★ ★ ★

Perfect Peter stood on the bench in the
front yard.

"Now say your line, 'I am too horrible
to live,' and jump off the bench into
the crocodile-filled moat, where you are
eaten alive and drown," said Henry.

"I don't want to say that," said Peter.

Horrid Henry lowered the camera.
"Do you want to be in the movie or
don't you?" he hissed.

17

"I am too horrible to live," muttered
Peter.

"Louder!" said Henry.

"I am too horrible to live," said Peter
a fraction louder.

"And as you drown, scream out, 'and
I have smelly pants,'" said Henry.

"*What?*" said Peter.

Tee-hee, thought Horrid Henry.

"But how come you get to play all
the other parts *and* dance *and* sing,
and all I get to do is walk around going

wooooooo?" said Susan sourly in next
door's yard.

"Because it's *my* movie," said Margaret.

"Keep it down, we're filming here,"
said Henry. "Now, Peter, you are
walking down the garden path out into
the street—"

"I thought I'd just drowned," said Peter.

Henry rolled his eyes.

"No, dummy, this is a horror movie.
You *rose* from the dead, and now you're
walking down the path singing this song,
just before the hairy scary monster leaps
out of the bushes and rips you to shreds.

**"Wibble bibble dribble pants
Bibble baby wibble pants
Wibble pants wibble pants
Dribble dribble dribble pants,"**

sang Horrid Henry.

Perfect Peter hesitated. "But, Henry, why would my character sing that song?"

Henry glared at Peter.

"Because I'm the director and I say so," said Henry.

Perfect Peter's lip trembled. He started walking.

"Wibble bibble dribble pants
Bibble baby wibble pants
Wibble pants wib–"

"I don't want to!" came a screech from next door's front yard.

"Susan, you *have* to be covered up in a sheet," said Margaret.

"But no one will see my face and know it's me," said Susan.

"Duh," said Margaret. "You're playing a ghost."

Sour Susan flung off the sheet.

"Well I quit," said Susan.

"You're fired!" shouted Margaret.

"I don't want to sing that dribble pants song," said Peter.

"Then you're fired!" screamed Henry.

"No!" screamed Perfect Peter. "I quit." And he ran out of the front gate, shrieking and wailing.

Wow, thought Horrid Henry. He chased after Peter, filming.

"I've had it!" screamed Sour Susan. "I don't want to be in your stupid movie!" She ran off down the road, shrieking and wailing.

Margaret chased after her, filming.

Cool, thought Horrid Henry, what a perfect end for his movie, the puny wimp running off terrified—

BUMP!

Susan and Peter collided and sprawled flat on the pavement.

CRASH!

Henry and Margaret tripped over the screaming Peter and Susan.

SMASH!

Horrid Henry dropped his camcorder.

SMASH!

Moody Margaret dropped *her*
camcorder.

OOPS.

Horrid Henry stared down at the
twisted broken metal as his monster
movie lay shattered on the concrete path.

WHOOPS.

Moody Margaret stared down at the
cracked camcorder as her Hollywood
horror movie lay in pieces on the ground.

"Henry!" hissed Margaret.

"Margaret!" hissed Henry.

"This is all your fault!" they wailed.

2

HORRID HENRY'S HORRID WEEKEND

"NOOOOOOOOO!" screamed Horrid Henry. "I don't want to spend the weekend with Steve."

"Don't be horrid, Henry," said Mom. "It's very kind of Aunt Ruby to invite us down for the weekend."

"But I hate Aunt Ruby!" shrieked Henry. "And I hate Steve and I hate you!"

"I can't wait to go," said Perfect Peter.

"Shut up, Peter!" howled Henry.

"Don't tell your brother to shut up," shouted Mom.

"Shut up! Shut up! Shut up!" And
Horrid Henry fell to the floor wailing
and screaming and kicking.

Stuck-Up Steve was Horrid Henry's
hideous cousin. Steve hated Henry.
Henry hated him. The last time Henry
had seen Steve, Henry had tricked
him into thinking there was a monster
under his bed. Steve had sworn revenge.
Then there was the other time at the
restaurant when…well, Horrid Henry
thought it would be a good idea to avoid
Steve until his cousin was grown-up and
in prison for crimes against humanity.

And now his mean, horrible parents were forcing him to spend a whole precious weekend with the toadiest, wormiest, smelliest boy who ever slimed out of a swamp.

Mom sighed. "We're going and that's that. Ruby says Steve is having a lovely friend over so that should be extra fun."

Henry stopped screaming and kicking. Maybe Steve's friend wouldn't be a stuck-up monster. Maybe *he'd* been forced to waste his weekend with Steve too. After all, who'd volunteer to spend time with Steve? Maybe together they could squish Stuck-Up Steve once and for all.

Ding dong.

Horrid Henry, Perfect Peter, Mom, and Dad stood outside Rich Aunt Ruby's enormous house on a gray, drizzly day. Steve opened the massive front door.

"Oh," he sneered. "It's you."

Steve opened the present Mom had brought. It was a small flashlight. Steve put it down.

"I already have a much better one," he said.

"Oh," said Mom.

Another boy stood beside him. A boy who looked vaguely familiar. A boy... Horrid Henry gasped. Oh no. It was Bill. Bossy Bill. The horrible son of Dad's boss. Henry had once tricked Bill into photocopying his bottom. Bill had sworn revenge. Horrid Henry's insides turned to jelly. Trust Stuck-Up Steve to be friends with Bossy Bill. It was bad enough being trapped in a house with one archenemy. Now he was stuck in a house with *two*...

Stuck-Up Steve scowled at Henry. "You're wearing that old shirt of mine," he said. "Don't your parents ever buy you new clothes?"

Bossy Bill snorted.

"Steve," said Aunt Ruby. "Don't be rude."

"I wasn't," said Steve. "I was just asking. No harm in asking, is there?"

"No," said Horrid Henry. He smiled at Steve. "So when will Aunt Ruby buy you a new face?"

"Henry," said Mom. "Don't be rude."

29

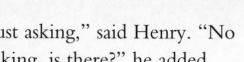

"I was just asking," said Henry. "No harm in asking, is there?" he added, glaring at Steve.

Steve glared back.

Aunt Ruby beamed. "Henry, Steve and Bill are taking you to their friend Tim's paintballing party."

"Won't that be fun," said Mom.

Peter looked frightened.

"Don't worry, Peter," said Aunt Ruby, "you can help me plant seedlings while the older boys are out."

Peter beamed. "Thank you," he said. "I don't like paintballing. Too messy and scary."

Paintballing! Horrid Henry loved paintballing. The chance to splat Steve and Bill with ooey gooey globs of paint...hmmm, maybe the weekend was looking up.

"Great!" said Horrid Henry.

"How nice," said Rich Aunt Ruby,
"you boys already know each other.
Think how much fun you're all going to
have sharing Steve's bedroom together."

Uh-oh, thought Horrid Henry.

"Yeah!" said Stuck-Up Steve. "We're
looking forward to sharing a room with
Henry." His piggy eyes gleamed.

"Yeah!" said Bossy Bill. "I can't wait."
His piggy eyes gleamed.

31

"Yeah," said Horrid Henry. He wouldn't be sleeping a wink.

Horrid Henry looked around the enormous high-ceilinged bedroom he'd be sharing with his two evil enemies for two very long days and one very long night. There was a bunk bed, which Steve and Bill had already nabbed, and two single beds. Steve's bedroom shelves were stuffed with zillions of new toys and games, as usual.

Bill and Steve smirked at each other. Henry scowled at them. What were they plotting?

"Don't you dare touch my Super-Blooper Blaster," said Steve.

"Don't you dare touch my Demon Dagger Saber," said Bill.

A Super-Blooper Blaster! A Demon Dagger Saber! Trust Bill and Steve to have the two best toys in the world…Rats.

"Don't worry," said Henry. "I don't play with baby toys."

"Oh yeah," said Stuck-Up Steve. "Bet you're too much of a baby to jump off my top bunk onto your bed."

"Am not," said Henry.

"We're not allowed to jump on beds," said Perfect Peter.

"We're not allowed," mimicked Steve. "I thought you were too poor to even *have* beds."

"Ha ha," said Henry.

"Chicken. Chicken. Scaredy-cat," sneered Bossy Bill.

"Squawk!" said Stuck-Up Steve. "I knew you'd be too scared, chicken."

That did it. *No* one called Horrid Henry chicken and lived. As if he, Henry, leader of a pirate gang, would be afraid to jump off a top bunk. Ha.

"Don't do it, Henry," said Perfect Peter.

"Shut up, worm," said Henry.

"But it's so high," squealed Peter, squeezing his eyes shut.

Horrid Henry clambered up the ladder and stepped onto the top bunk. "It's nothing," he lied. "I've jumped off *much* higher."

"Well, go on then," said Stuck-Up
Steve.

Boing! Horrid Henry bounced.

Boing! Horrid Henry bounced higher.
Whee! This bed was very springy.

"We're waiting, chicken," said Bossy
Bill.

BOING! BOING! Horrid Henry bent
his knees, then—leap! He jumped onto
the single bed below.

SMASH!

Horrid Henry
crashed
to the floor
as the bed
collapsed
beneath him.

Huh? What? How
could he have broken
the bed? He hadn't heard any
breaking sounds. It was as if...as if...

35

Mom, Dad, and Aunt Ruby ran into the room.

"Henry broke the bed," said Stuck-Up Steve.

"We tried to stop him," said Bossy Bill, "but Henry insisted on jumping."

"But…but…" said Horrid Henry.

"Henry!" wailed Mom. "You horrid boy."

"How could you be so horrid?" said Dad. "No allowance for a year. Ruby, I'm so sorry."

Aunt Ruby pursed her lips. "These things happen," she said.

"And no paintballing party for you," said Mom.

What?

"No!" wailed Henry.

Then Horrid Henry saw a horrible sight. Behind Aunt Ruby's back, Steve and Bill were covering their mouths and

laughing. Henry realized the terrible
truth. Bill and Steve had tricked him.

They'd broken the bed. And now *he'd*
gotten the blame.

"But I didn't break it!" screamed Henry.

"Yes you did, Henry," said Peter. "I
saw you."

AAAARRRRGGGGHHHH! Horrid
Henry leaped at Peter. He was a storm
god hurling thunderbolts at a foolish
mortal.

"AAAIIIEEEEEE!" squealed Perfect
Peter.

"Henry! Stop it!" shrieked Mom. "Leave your brother alone."

Nah nah ne nah nah mouthed Steve behind Aunt Ruby's back.

"Isn't it lovely how nicely the boys are playing together?" said Aunt Ruby.

"Yes, isn't it?" said Mom.

"Not surprising," said Aunt Ruby, beaming. "After all, Steve is such a polite, friendly boy, I've never met anyone who didn't love him."

Snore! Snore! Snore!

Horrid Henry lay on a mattress listening to hideous snoring sounds. He'd stayed awake for hours, just in case they tried anything horrible, like pouring water on his head, or stuffing frogs in his bed. Which was what he was going to do to Peter, the moment he got home.

Henry had just spent the most horrible Saturday of his life. He'd begged to go to the paintballing party. He'd pleaded to go to the paintballing party. He'd screamed about going to the paintballing party. But no. His mean, horrible parents wouldn't budge. And it was all Steve and Bill's fault. They'd tripped him going down the stairs.

They'd kicked him under the table at lunch (and then complained that he was kicking *them*). And every time Aunt

Ruby's back was turned they stuck out their tongues and jeered: "We're going paintballing and you're not."

He had to get to that party. And he had to be revenged. But how? How? His two archenemies had banded together and struck the first blow. Could he booby-trap their beds and remove a few slats? Unfortunately, everyone would know *he'd* done it and he'd be in even more trouble than he was now.

Scare them? Tell them there was a monster under the bed? Hmmm. He knew Steve was as big a scaredy-cat as Peter. But he'd already done that once. He didn't think Steve would fall for it again.

Get them into trouble? Turn them against each other? Steal their best toys and hide them? Hmmm. Hmmm.

Horrid Henry thought and thought.
He had to be revenged. He had to.

Tweet tweet. It was Sunday morning.
The birds were singing. The sun was
shining. The—

Yank!

Bossy Bill and Stuck-Up Steve pulled
off his blanket.

"Nah na ne nah nah, we-ee beat
you," crowed Bill.

"Nah na ne nah nah, we got you into
trouble," crowed Steve.

Horrid Henry scowled. Time to put
Operation Revenge into action.

"Bill thinks you're bossy, Steve," said
Henry. "He told me."

"Did not," said Bossy Bill.

"And Steve thinks you're stuck-up,
Bill," added Henry sweetly.

"No, I don't," said Steve.

"Then why'd you tell me that?" said Horrid Henry.

Steve stuck his nose in the air. "Nice try, Henry, you big loser," said Stuck-Up Steve. "Just ignore him, Bill."

"Henry, it's not nice to tell lies," said Perfect Peter.

"Shut up, worm," snarled Horrid Henry.

Rats.

Time for plan B.

Except he didn't have a plan B.

"I can't wait for Tim's party," said Bossy Bill. "You never know what's going to happen."

"Yeah, remember when he told us he was having a pirate party and instead we went to the Wild West Theme Park!" said Steve.

"Or when he said we were having a sleepover, and instead we all went to a Manic Buzzards concert."

"And Tim gives the best party bags. Last year everyone got a Deluxe Demon Dagger Saber," said Steve. "Wonder what he'll give this year? Oh, I forgot, Henry won't be coming to the party."

"Too bad you can't come, Henry," sneered Bossy Bill.

"Yeah, too bad," sneered Stuck-Up Steve. "Not."

ARRRRGGGHH. Horrid Henry's blood boiled. He couldn't decide what was worse, listening to them crow about having gotten him into so much trouble or brag about the great party they were going to and he wasn't.

"I can't wait to find out what surprises he'll have in store this year," said Bill.

"Yeah," said Steve.

Who cares? thought Horrid Henry. Unless Tim was planning to throw Bill and Steve into a shark tank. That would be a nice surprise. Unless of course…

And then suddenly Horrid Henry had a brilliant, spectacular idea. It was so brilliant and so spectacular, that for a moment he wondered whether he could stop himself from flinging open the window and shouting his plan out loud. Oh wow. Oh wow. It was risky. It was dangerous. But if it worked, he would have the best revenge ever in the history of the world. No, the history of the solar system. No, the history of the universe!

It was an hour before the party. Horrid Henry was counting the seconds until he could escape.

Aunt Ruby popped her head around the door waving an envelope.

"Letter for you boys," she said.

Steve snatched it and tore it open.

Dear Steve and Bill
Party of the year update.
Everyone must come to my house
wearing pajamas (you'll find
out why later, but don't be
surprised if we all end up in
a movie – shhhh). It'll be a real
laugh. Make sure to bring
your favorite soft toys too,
and wear your fluffiest
slippers. Hollywood, here
we come!

Tim

"He must be planning something *amazing*," said Bill.

"I bet we're all going to be acting in a movie!" said Steve.

"Yeah!" said Bill.

"Too bad *you* won't, Henry," said Stuck-Up Steve.

"You're so lucky," said Henry. "I wish I were going."

Mom looked at Dad.

Dad looked at Mom.

Henry held his breath.

"Well, you can't, Henry, and that's final," said Mom.

"It's so unfair!" shrieked Henry.

Henry's parents dropped Steve and Bill off at Tim's party on their way home. Steve was in his blue bunny pajamas and blue bunny fluffy slippers and clutching a panda.

Bill was in his yellow duckling pajamas and yellow duckling fluffy slippers and clutching his monkey.

"Shame you can't come, Henry," said

Steve, smirking. "But we'll be sure to
tell you all about it."

"Do," said Henry as Mom drove off.

Horrid Henry heard squeals of laughter
at Hoity-Toity Tim's front door. Bill and
Steve stood frozen. Then they started to
wave frantically at the car.

"Are they saying something?" said
Mom, glancing in the rearview mirror.

"Nah, just waving good-bye," said Horrid Henry. He rolled down his window.

"Have fun, guys!"

3

HORRID HENRY'S GRUMP CARD

"I've been so good!" shrieked Horrid Henry. "Why can't I have a grump card?"

"You have not been good," said Mom.

"You've been awful," said Dad.

"No, I haven't," said Henry.

Mom sighed. "Just today you pinched Peter and called him names. You pushed him off the comfy black chair. You screamed. You wouldn't eat your sprouts. You—"

"Aside from *that*," said Horrid Henry. "I've been *so* good. I deserve a grump card."

"Henry," said Dad. "You know we only give grump cards for *exceptionally* good behavior."

"But I never get one!" howled Henry.

Mom and Dad looked at each other.

"And why do you think that is?" said Mom.

"Because you're mean and unfair and the worst parents in the world!" screamed Horrid Henry.

What other reason could there be?

A grump card was precious beyond gold and silver and rubies and diamonds. If Mom or Dad thought you'd behaved totally spectacularly above and beyond the call of duty they gave you a grump card. A grump card meant that you could erase any future punishment. A grump card was a glittering, golden, get-out-of-jail-free ticket.

Horrid Henry had never had a grump

card. Just think, if he had even one…if
Dad was in the middle of telling him
off, or banning him from the computer
for a week, all Henry had to do was
hand him a grump card, and, like
magic, the telling off would end, the
punishment would be erased, and
Henry would be back on the computer
zapping baddies.

Horrid Henry longed for a grump
card. But how could he ever get one?

Even Peter, who was always perfect, only had seven. And he'd never even used a single one. What a waste. What a total waste.

Imagine what he could do if he had a grump card…He could scoff every sweet and cookie and treat in the house. He could forget all about homework and watch TV instead. And best of all, if Dad ever tried to ban him from the computer or Mom shouted that he'd lost his allowance for a month, all Henry had to do was produce the magic card.

What bliss.

What heaven.

What joy.

But *how* could Henry get a grump card? How? How?

Could he behave totally exceptionally above and beyond the call of duty?

Horrid Henry considered. Nah.
That was impossible. He'd once spent
a whole day being perfect, and
even then had ended up being sent to
his room.

So how else to get a grump card?

Steal one? Hmmm. Tempting. Very
tempting. He could sneak into Peter's
room, snatch a grump card or two, then
sneak out again. He could even
substitute a fake grump card at the
bottom in case Peter noticed his stash

was smaller. But then Peter would be sure to tell on him when Henry produced the golden ticket to freedom, and Mom and Dad would be so mad they'd probably *double* his punishment and ban him from the computer for life.

Or he could kidnap Fluff Puff, Peter's favorite plastic sheep, and hold

 him for ransom. Yes! And then when Peter had ransomed him back, Henry could steal him again. And again. Until all Peter's grump cards were his. Yes! He was brilliant. He was a genius. Why had he never thought of this before?

Except…if Peter told on him, Henry had a horrible feeling that he would get into trouble. Big, big trouble that

56

not even a grump card could get him
out of.

Time to think again. Could he swap
something for one? What did Henry
have that Peter wanted? Comics? No.
Chips? No. Killer Boy Rats CDs?
No way.

Henry sighed. Maybe he could *buy*
one from Peter. Unfortunately, Horrid
Henry never had any money. Whatever
pitiful allowance he ever had always
seemed to vanish through his fingers.
Besides, who'd want to give that wormy
worm a penny?

Better yet, could Henry *trick* Peter
into giving him one? Yeah! They could
play a great game called Learn to Share.
Henry could tell Peter to give him
half his grump cards as Peter needed to
learn to stop being such a selfish hog. It
could work...

There was a snuffling sound, like a pig rustling for truffles, and Perfect Peter stuck his head around the door.

"What are you doing, Henry?" asked Peter.

"None of your business, worm," said Horrid Henry.

"Want to play with me?" said Peter.

"No," said Henry. Peter was always nagging Henry to play with him. But when Henry had played Robot and Mad Professor with him, for some reason Peter hadn't enjoyed giving Henry all his candy and money and doing all Henry's chores for him.

"We could play checkers...or Scrabble?" said Peter.

"N-O spells no," said Henry. "Now get out of—" Horrid Henry paused. Wait a minute. Wait a minute...

"How much will you pay me?" said Horrid Henry.

Perfect Peter stared at Henry.

"Pay you? *Pay* you to play with me?"

"Yeah," said Henry.

Perfect Peter considered.

"How much?" said Peter slowly.

"One dollar a minute," said Henry.

"One dollar a minute!" said Peter.

"It's a good offer, toad," said Henry.

"No, it isn't," said Peter.

"What, you think it should be two dollars a minute?" said Henry. "Okay."

"I'm going to tell on you," said Peter.

"Tell what, worm? That I made you a perfectly good offer? No one's forcing you."

Perfect Peter paused. Henry was right. He could just say no.

"Or…" said Horrid Henry. "You could pay me in grump cards."

"Grump cards?" said Peter.

"After all, you have tons and you never use them," said Henry. "You could spare one or two or four and never notice…and you'll refill your stash in no time."

It was true that he didn't really need his grump cards, thought Peter. And it would be so nice to play a game…

"Okay," said Peter.

YES! thought Horrid Henry. What a genius he was.

"I charge one grump card a minute."

"No," said Peter. "Grump cards are valuable."

Horrid Henry sighed.

"Tell you what, because I'm such a nice brother, I will play you a game of Scra…Scrab…" Horrid Henry could barely bring himself to even say the word *Scrabble*…"for two grump cards. And a game of checkers for two more."

"And a stuffed animal tea party?" said Peter.

Did anyone suffer as much as Henry? He sighed loudly.

"Okay," said Horrid Henry. "But that'll cost you three."

Horrid Henry stared happily at his seven glorious grump cards. He'd done it! He was free to do anything he wanted. He would be king forever.

Why wait?

Horrid Henry skipped downstairs,
went straight to the candy jar, and took
a huge handful of candy.

"Put those back, Henry," said Mom.
"You know candy day is Saturday."

"Don't care," said Henry. "I want
candy now and I'm having them now."
Shoving the huge handful into his
mouth, he reached into the jar for more.

"Henry!" screamed Mom. "Put those
back. That's it. No candy for a week.
Now go straight—"

Horrid Henry whipped out a grump card and handed it to Mom.

Mom gasped. Her jaw dropped.

"Where…when…did you get a grump card?"

Henry shrugged. "I got it 'cause I was so good."

Mom stared at him. Dad must have given him one. How amazing.

Henry strolled into the living room. Time for *Terminator Gladiator*!

Dad was sitting on the sofa watching the boring news. Well, not for long. Horrid Henry grabbed the clicker and switched channels.

"Hey," said Dad. "I was watching."

"Tough," said Henry. "I'm watching what I want to watch. Go, Gladiator!" he squealed.

"Don't be horrid, Henry. I'm warning you…"

Horrid Henry stuck out his tongue at Dad. "Buzz off, baldie."

Dad gasped.

"That's it, Henry. No computer games for a week. Now go straight—"

Dad stared at the grump card that Henry waved at him. Henry? A grump card? Mom must have given him one. But how? When?

"I'll just go off now and play on the computer," said Henry, smirking.

Tee-hee. The look on Dad's face. And what fun to play on the computer, after he'd been banned from it! That was well worth a grump card. After all, he had plenty.

★ ★ ★

Horrid Henry spat his sprouts onto
the floor. But a grump card took care
of the "no TV for the rest of the day"
punishment. Then he flicked peas at Peter
and nicked four of his fries. That was
well worth a grump card, too, thought
Horrid Henry, to get his allowance
back. Bit of a shame that he had to give
two grump cards to lift the ban on going
to Ralph's sleepover, but, hey, that's
what grump cards were for, right?

"Henry, it's my turn to play on the
computer," said Peter.

"Tough," said Horrid Henry, zapping
and blasting.

"I'm going to tell on you," said Peter.

"Go ahead," said Henry. "See if I care."

"You're going to get into big, big
trouble," said Peter.

"Go away, wormy worm toady pants poopsicle," said Henry. "You're annoying me."

"Mom! Henry just called me a wormy worm toady pants poopsicle!" shrieked Peter.

"Henry! Stop calling your brother names," said Mom.

"I didn't," shouted Henry.

"He did too!" howled Peter.

"Shut up, Ugg-face!" snarled Henry.

"Mom! Henry just called me Ugg-face!"

"That's it," said Mom. "Henry! Go to your room. No computer for a—"

Horrid Henry handed over another grump card.

"Henry. Where did you get these?" said Mom.

"I was given them for being good,"

said Horrid Henry. That wasn't a lie,
because he had been good by playing
with Peter, and Peter had given them
to him.

Perfect Peter burst into tears.

"Henry tricked me," said Peter. "He
took my grump cards."

"Did not."

"Did too."

"We made a deal, you wibble-face

68

nappy!" shrieked Henry and attacked. He was a bulldozer flattening a wriggling worm...

"AAARRRGGGHH!" screamed Peter.

"You horrid boy," said Mom. "No allowance for a week. No TV for a week. No computer for a week. No candy for a week. Go to your room!"

Whoa, grump card to the rescue. Thank goodness he'd saved one for emergencies.

What? Huh?

Horrid Henry felt frantically inside his
pockets. He looked on the floor. He
checked his pockets again. And again.
There were no grump cards left.

What had he done? Had he just
blown all his grump cards in an hour?
His precious, precious grump cards?

The grump cards he'd never, ever get again?

NOOOOOOOOO!!!!!!!

4

HORRID HENRY'S OLYMPICS

Chomp chomp chomp chomp…Burp. Ahhh! Horrid Henry scoffed the last crumb of Super Spicy Hedgehog chips and burped again. So yummy. Wow. He'd eaten the entire pack in seventeen seconds. No one could guzzle chips faster than Horrid Henry, especially when he was having to gobble them secretly in class. He'd never been caught, not even—

A dark, icy shadow fell across him.

"Are you eating in class, Henry?" hissed Miss Battle-Axe.

"No," said Henry.

Tee-hee. Thanks to his super-speedy jaws, he'd already swallowed the evidence.

"Then where did this chip packet come from?" said Miss Battle-Axe, pointing to the plastic bag on the floor.

Henry shrugged.

"Bert! Is this yours?"

"I dunno," said Beefy Bert.

"There is no eating in class," said Miss Battle-Axe. Why did she have to say the same things over and over? One day the Queen would discover that she, Boudicca Battle-Axe, was her long-lost daughter and sweep her off to the palace, where she would live a life of pampered luxury. But until then—

"Now, as I was saying, before I was so rudely interrupted," she glared at Horrid Henry, "our school will be having its very own Olympics.

We'll be running and jumping and
swimming and—"

"Eating!" yelled Horrid Henry.

"Quiet, Henry," snapped Miss Battle-
Axe. "I want all of you to practice hard,
both in school and out, to show—"

Horrid Henry stopped listening. It was
so unfair. Wasn't it bad enough that every
morning he had to heave his heavy
bones out of bed to go to school, without

wasting any of his precious TV-watching time running and jumping and swimming? He was a terrible runner. He was a pathetic jumper. He was a hopeless swimmer—though he did have his five-meter badge…Besides, Aerobic Al was sure to win every medal. In fact, they should just give them all to him now and save everyone else a load of bother.

Shame, thought Horrid Henry, that the things he was so good at never got prizes. If there was a medal for who could watch TV the longest or who could eat the most candy, or who was quickest out of the classroom door when the last bell rang, well, he'd be covered in gold from head to toe.

"Go on, Susan! Jump higher."

"I'm jumping as high as I can," said Sour Susan.

"That's not high," said Moody
Margaret. "A tortoise could jump higher
than you."

"Then get a tortoise," snapped Susan
sourly.

"You're just a lazy lump."
"You're just a moody meanie."
"Lump."
"Meanie."
"LUMP!"

"MEANIE!"

Slap!

Slap!

"Whatcha doin'?" asked Horrid Henry, leaning over the garden wall.

"Go away, Henry," said Margaret.

"Yeah, Henry," said Susan.

"I can stand in my own yard if I want to," said Henry.

"Just ignore him," said Margaret.

"We're practicing for the school Olympics," said Susan.

Horrid Henry snorted.

"I don't see *you* practicing," said Margaret.

"That's 'cause I'm doing my *own* Olympics, frog-face," said Henry.

His jaw dropped. YES! YES! A thousand times yes! Why hadn't he thought of this before? Of course he should set up his own Olympics.

And have the competitions he'd always wanted to have. A name-calling competition! A chocolate-eating competition!

A chip-eating competition! A who-could-watch-the-most-TVs-at-the-same-time-competition! He'd make sure he had competitions that *he* could win. The Henry Olympics. The Holympics. And the prizes would be… the prizes would be… masses and masses of chocolate!

"Can Ted and Gordon

and I be in your Olympics?"
said Perfect Peter.

"NO!" said
Henry. Who'd
want some nappy
babies competing?
They'd spoil
everything, they'd—

Wait a minute…

"Of course you can, Peter," said
Henry smoothly. "That will be one
dollar each."

"Why?" said Ted.

"To pay for the super fantastic prizes,
of course," said Henry. "Each champion
will win a massive prize of…chocolate!"

Peter's face fell.

"Oh," he said.

"And a medal," added Henry quickly.

"Oh," said Peter, beaming.

"How massive?" said Margaret.

"Armfuls and armfuls," said Horrid Henry. His mouth watered just thinking about it.

"Hmmm," said Margaret. "Well, I think there should be a speed haircutting competition. And dancing."

"Dancing?" said Henry. Well, why not? He was a marvelous dancer. His elephant stomp would win any competition hands down. "Okay."

Margaret and Susan plonked down one dollar each.

"By the way, that's *ballroom* dancing," said Margaret.

"No way," said Henry.

"No ballroom dancing, then we won't enter," said Margaret. "And Linda and Gurinder and Kate and Fiona and Soraya won't either."

Horrid Henry considered. He was sure to win everything else, so why not let her have a tiny victory? And the more people who entered, the more chocolate for him!

"Okay," said Henry.

"Bet you're scared I'll win everything," said Margaret.

"Am not."

"Are too."

"I can eat more candy than you any day."

"Ha!" said Margaret. "I'd like to see you try."

"The Purple Hand Gang can beat the Secret Club *and* the Best Boys

Club, no sweat," said Horrid Henry.
"Bring it on."

★ ★ ★

THE REAL OLYMPICS ARE HERE!

TIRED OF BORING OLD SWIMMING AND RUNNING? OF COURSE YOU ARE!

NOW'S YOUR CHANCE TO COMPETE IN THE

HOLYMPICS

THE GREATEST OLYMPICS OF ALL!!!
SPEED-EATING CANDY! TV WATCHING!
CHIP EATING! BURP TO THE BEAT!

BALLROOM DANCING. SPEED HAIRCUTTING.

Entry Fee $1 for the chance to win loads of chocolate!!!!!

"Hang on," said Margaret. "What's with calling this the Holympics? It should be the Molympics. I came up with the haircutting and dancing competitions."

"'Cause Molympics is a terrible name," said Henry.

"So's Holympics," said Margaret.

"Actually," said Peter, "I think it should be called the Polympics."

"Shut up, worm," said Henry.

"Yeah, worm," said Margaret.

"Mom!" screamed Henry. "*Mom!!!!!!!!*"

Mom came running out of the shower.

"What is it, Henry?" she said, dripping water all over the floor. "Are you all right?"

"I need candy," he said.

"You got me out of the shower because you need candy?" she repeated.

"I need to practice for the candy speed-eating competition," said Henry. "For my Olympics."

"Absolutely not," said Mom.

Horrid Henry was outraged.

"How am I supposed to win if I can't practice?" he howled. "You're always telling me to practice stuff. And now when I want to you won't let me."

Bookings for Henry's Olympics were brisk. Everyone in Henry's class—and a

few from Peter's—wanted to compete.
Horrid Henry gazed happily at the
45 dollars' worth of chocolate and chips
piled high on his bed. Wow. Wow.
Mega mega wow. Boxes and boxes
and boxes filled with yummy, yummy
sweets! Giant bar after giant bar of
chocolate. His Holympics would have
the best prizes ever. And he, Henry,
fully expected to win most of them.
He'd win enough chocolate to last him
a lifetime *and* have the glory of coming
first, for once.

Horrid Henry gazed at the chocolate
prize mountain.

The chocolate prize mountain gazed
back at him and winked.

Wait.

He, Henry, was doing *all* the work.
Surely it was only fair if he got *something*
for his valuable time. He should have

kept a bit of money
back to cover his
expenses.

Horrid Henry
removed a giant
chocolate bar from
the pile.

After all, I do need
to practice for the
speed-eating contest, he
thought, tearing off the
wrapper and shoving a
massive piece into his

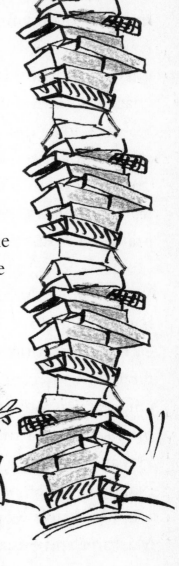

mouth. And then another. Oh boy, was that chocolate yummy. In a few seconds, it was gone.

Yeah! Horrid Henry, chocolate-eating champion of the universe!

You know, thought Henry, gazing at the chocolate mound teetering precariously on his bed, I think I bought *too* many prizes. And I *do* need to practice for my event...

What a great day, thought Horrid Henry happily. He'd won the candy speed-eating competition (though Greedy Graham had come a close second), the chip-eating contest *and* the name-calling one. (Peter had run off screaming when Henry called him Wibble Wobble Pants, Nappy Noodle, and Odiferous.)

Rude Ralph won "Burp to the Beat." Margaret and Susan won best ballroom dancers. Vain Violet was the surprise winner of the speed haircutting competition. Weepy William…well, his hair would grow back—eventually.

Best of all, Aerobic Al didn't win a thing.

The winners gathered around to collect their prizes.

"Where's my chocolate, Henry?" said Moody Margaret.

"And there better be loads like you promised," said Vain Violet.

Horrid Henry reached into the big prize bag.

Now, where was the ballroom dancing prize?

He pulled out a Choco Bloco. Yikes, was that all the chocolate he had left? He rummaged around some more.

"A Choco Bloco?" said Margaret slowly. "A *single* Choco Bloco?"

"They're very yummy," said Henry.

"And mine?" said Violet.

"And mine?" said Ralph.

"And mine for coming second?" said Graham.

"You're supposed to share it!" screamed Horrid Henry, as he turned and ran.

Wow, thought Horrid Henry, as he fled down the

road, Rude Ralph, Moody Margaret, Sour Susan, Vain Violet, and Greedy Graham chasing after him, I'm pretty fast when I need to be. Maybe I *should* enter the school Olympics after all.

Acknowledgments

Thanks to Imogen Stubbs
for sharing some fine filmmaking
moments with me.

The HORRID HENRY books
by Francesca Simon

Illustrated by Tony Ross

Each book contains four stories

HORRID HENRY AND THE ZOMBIE VAMPIRE

Horrid Henry writes the best story ever, spars with a famous chef over his school's lunch menu, creates a new game with Perfect Peter, and hunts for zombie vampires.

HORRID HENRY
WAKES THE DEAD

Horrid Henry plots a brilliant plan for total TV control; schemes, bribes, and fights his way to become class president; battles with Peter over who gets the awesome purple dinosaur and who's stuck with the boring green one; and performs the greatest magic trick the world has ever seen at his school's talent contest.

HORRID HENRY ROCKS

Horrid Henry invades Perfect Peter's room; hunts for cookies in Moody Margaret's Secret Club tent, with frightening results; writes his biography— and Moody Margaret's; and plots to see the best band in the world (while his family wants to see the worst).

HORRID HENRY AND
THE ABOMINABLE SNOWMAN

Horrid Henry builds the biggest, meanest
monster snowman ever; writes his will (but
is more interested in what others should be
leaving him); starts his own makeover
business; and manages to thwart the Happy
Nappy for a chance
to meet his favorite
author in the
whole world.

HORRID HENRY'S UNDERPANTS

Horrid Henry discovers a genius way to write thank-you letters; negotiates over vegetables; competes with Perfect Peter over which of them is sickest; and finds himself wearing the wrong underpants—with dreadful consequences.

HORRID HENRY

Henry is dragged to dancing class against his will; vies with Moody Margaret to make the yuckiest Glop; goes camping; and tries to be good like Perfect Peter— but not for long.

About the Author

Photo: Francesco Guidicini

Francesca Simon spent her childhood on the beach in California and then went to Yale and Oxford Universities to study medieval history and literature. She now lives in London with her family. She has written over forty-five books and won the Children's Book of the Year in 2008 at the Galaxy British Book Awards for *Horrid Henry and the Abominable Snowman*.